jE

c.1

Library of Congress Cataloging in Publication Data
Vincent, Gabrielle.   Ernest and Celestine.
Translation of: Ernest et Célestine ont perdu Siméon.
Summary: Ernest, a bear, and Celestine, a mouse,
lose Celestine's stuffed bird in the snow.
[1. Animals – Fiction.   2. Toys – Fiction]   PZ7.V744Er   [E]
ISBN 0-688-00855-0   81-6392
ISBN 0-688-00856-9 (lib. bdg.)   AACR2

AUG '82

CL

GABRIELLE VINCENT
Ernest and Celestine

GREENWILLOW BOOKS, New York

"Come on, Gideon. We're going for a walk."

"Wait a minute, Ernest. We're almost ready."

"Let's go back, Celestine. It's too cold."

"Ernest! I've lost Gideon!"

"It's too dark, Celestine. We'll never find him now."

"It's all your fault, Ernest!"

"Please don't cry, Celestine. We'll find him in the morning."

"Oh, poor Gideon. How will I tell Celestine?"

"Let's see ..."

"A green beak?"

"But there wasn't one like Gideon."

"I want Gideon."

"Celestine, I've got an idea."

"Draw his feet carefully."

"Don't come in. Wait until I'm finished."

"Oh, Gideon!"

"We'll have a party to celebrate. A Christmas party for Gideon."

"We'll see you tonight."

"That's enough. Go to sleep now."

"Are you going to help me with the dishes?"

"Oh, Ernest! I'll help you any time!"